Little Wolf,
Forest Detective

Also by Ian Whybrow
and illustrated by Tony Ross

Little Wolf's Book of Badness
Little Wolf's Diary of Daring Deeds
Little Wolf's Haunted Hall for Small Horrors
Little Wolf's Postbag

Little Wolf's website address is:
www.littlewolf.co.uk

First published in Great Britain by Collins in 2000
First published in paperback by Collins in 2001
Collins is an imprint of HarperCollins*Publishers* Ltd
77-85 Fulham Palace Road, Hammersmith, London W6 8JB

The HarperCollins website address is www.**fire**and**water**.com

3 5 7 9 8 6 4 2

Text copyright © Ian Whybrow 2000
Illustrations copyright © Tony Ross 2000

ISBN 0 00 675452 X

The author and illustrator assert the moral right to
be identified as author and illustrator of the work.

Printed and bound in Great Britain by
Omnia Books Limited, Glasgow

Little Wolf, Forest Detective

Ian Whybrow

Illustrated by Tony Ross

Collins

An imprint of HarperCollinsPublishers

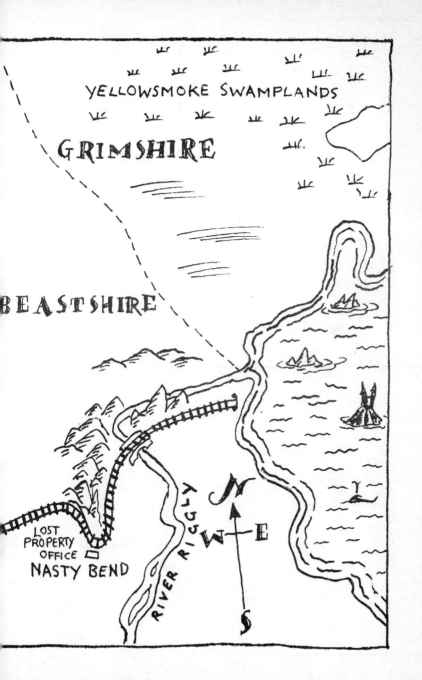

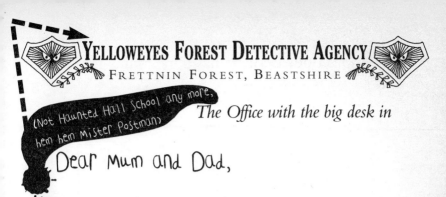

(Not Haunted Hall School any more, hem hem Mister Postman)

The Office with the big desk in

Dear Mum and Dad,

Please please please PLEEEZ don't make me come home to Murkshire to live in the Lair with you and Smells. Whyo Y can't I stay here in Frettnin Forest with Yeller, Stubbs and Normus? Because we like being detectives, it is good. Stubbs has made us posh badges with his clever beak like this saying YFDA (for Yelloweyes Forest Detective Agency, did you know that?).

Also on our door he has done a nice new ~~sing sine~~ notice saying:

CHEEF DETECTIVES
Little B Wolf
plus Yeller Wolf (best friend and cuz)
FLYING SQUAD
Stubby Crow, Arksquire
BIG TUFF CLUE HUNTER
Normus Bear

We are good solvers but not Smells. His brane is 2 small plus he did not want to be in the YFDA. He got all feddup and lairsick remember? That is Y he came back to Murkshire to live in the Lair with you, then he could be your darling baby pet, yes? So not my fault.

Go on, make him stay there, we do not want him back, messing up our detective stuff. Like sitting on the fingerprint pad and doing bottomprints on my notebook. Also, he is selfish saying nobody else can be the handcuffer, only him.

Go on.

Yours hopingly,

Little Wolf

My room

Dear Mum and Dad,

You did not say much to my last letter, only hmmph and grrrr, and where is Uncle Bigbad's ghost? Find him quick or else!!!

We have been looking and looking, only no luck yet. Still, I have done you nice pics of what's in our detective kit so you will get more cheery. Yeller sent off for it to *Wolf Weekly* (cheap). It is like this:

DETECTIVE KIT

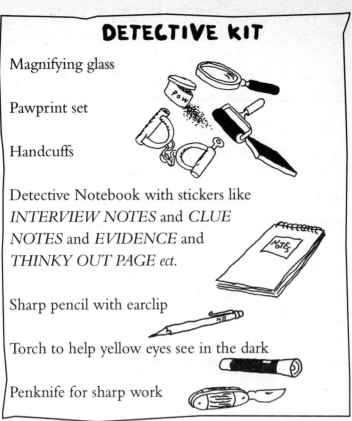

Magnifying glass

Pawprint set

Handcuffs

Detective Notebook with stickers like
INTERVIEW NOTES and *CLUE
NOTES* and *EVIDENCE* and
THINKY OUT PAGE ect.

Sharp pencil with earclip

Torch to help yellow eyes see in the dark

Penknife for sharp work

By the way, you say what new cases have we
got to solve, grrrr? Answer, allsorts but
confidenshul, privat, can't say anything hem hem.

Yours acely,

L B Wolf

Co-Cheef Detective, YFDA

Dear Mamong et Parp-parp (french),

No we have not found Mister Twister yet. Yes, I do remember he has shamed the name of Wolf by being a kidnapper and ghostnapping Uncle Bigbad in his whisky bottle. But do not fret and frown, we will solve this case soonly, easy cheesy. (Probly.) But just now we are a bit busy doing Tips for Tecs to help us. Do you like them?

TIPS FOR FOREST TECS

- *practise magnifying, pawprinting, handcuffing, sharpening (pencils) and shortpaw writing*

- *Use your brute instinct*

- *Use your keen beastly senses, such as eyes, ears, nose, also having a good lick*

👣 *Find clues*

👣 *Write about them in your notebook quick but no smudjis*

👣 *Have a good think*

👣 *Do plans for fast getaways*

Then you will be Mister ACE Forest Detective and case solver, arrroooo!

Good, eh?

Yours cheefly,

L Wolf (son)

Shadow of my best tree

Dear Mum and Dad,

You keep saying what is the point of being your son if I do not blab my secret cases to my mum and dad? Oh OK then, I will say about just 1, but keep it in the Lair. It is called The Case of the Ants' Lost Football Boots. Now I will say about the solving part.

The captain of Ants United FC came under our office door wearing his captain's strip with his number on (Number 9999999). He said antly, "Hello, somebody has pinched all my team's football boots, can you detect who dunnit?" Normus said, "Yes and I will bash them up for you." But me and Yeller and Stubbs said, "No need for bashing, Normus. Just adding up, plus using your keen beastly senses."

So Normus said, "Right then, how many boots got pinched?" and the captain said, "All the lot." That was a hard sum to add up, because of ants having to times by loads of feet. But Yeller got the answer, 6 x 11= 66. Then Normus said to the ant, "Hoy, have you got any reserves?"

Good thing he said that because the answer was yes, 1. That made 72 boots pinched. And guess what? We solved who the stealer was! Arrrooo for the YFDA!

And now:

NEW MYSTERY CRIMES OF FRETTNIN FOREST

1) 13 pups, chicks, cubs, fledgies
ect. have gone missing from
Frettnin Forest in 2 days

2) Also much treasure keeps getting robbed

3) Reports coming in of
strange spookly small
things seen in the night

Good. Because that means loads more
detecting for us. So watch out all you
kidnappers and robberers and small spookles,
because we have a detective kit and we can
find out WHODUNNIT!

Yours trackingly,

L B Wolf

Co·cheef Detective, YFDA

Under dinner table (for cosyness, hmmm)

Dear Mum and Dad,

About *The Case of the Ants' Lost Football Boots*, I forgot to finish off, sorry. The solving part was, we got out our magnifying glasses and had a good look round the heap where the ants live, going stare stare.

Anycase, quite soonly, we found many a small track. We followed these, crawlingly, to a rotted log. And guess what we found hiding under the bark? A centipede wearing 72 football boots! Stubbs can speak Insect so he said, "Ark Squark Crark?" ect. meaning arkscuse me, small crook, are you warking for Mister Twister the Farks? Or are you warking alone as a stealer? Also have you seen the ghost of Bigbad Wolf in a whisky bottle by any small chance?

The centipede said (insect voice), "It is a fair cop, misters. But I have not seen a big bad ghost and no I do not work for Mister Twister. Also, I am not a crook really. I just wanted to do loud riverdancing and get faymuss. By the way I taste horrible, hint hint."

Then he tried to do a fast getaway but no, he tripped over his laces and got captured har har. So well done us.

Yours Xplainingly

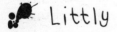 Littly

PS He Xcaped soonly, boo shame. Must get smaller handcuffs.

Dear Mum and Dad,

We had a good wet hunt for Mister Twister
and Uncle Bigbad's ghost today, so I bet you
are going pat pat well done our cub. Yeller's
Big Ideer was to swim down and look at Lake
Lemming's bottom. Because you never know,
Mister Twister is crafty enuff to hide down
there. We saw some nice bubbles, also
Normus caught a nice fishy tea (yum yum
tasty). But no crooks or ghosts in whisky
bottles, boo shame.

The ants' football team came over today saying we can be best friends and they will give us a kick-about any time. Good, eh? Also, today we got a hansum reward because we found a lost froghopper in the long grass and took him back to his mum. She was so happy, she gave us some cuckoo spit. So now we have got some nice froth to go on cups of hot choclit, yum yum tasty!

Yours yawnly,

Laaah Waaaah Zzzzzzz

Dear Mum and Dad,

It is not my fault Smells is jealous of my adventures. He always gets jealous. So go on, make him stay with you, hmmm? stroke stroke. Also, you are not fair, saying grrrrr you bet we do not earn much money being detectives because we cannot find my own dead uncle even. True we are not rich yet, BUT (big but) what about all that gold I had in my safe till Smellybreff got some gunpowder and blew it to small smithers? That made my gold go scattering all over Frettnin Forest.

Never mind, guess what? Stubbs found 3 gold coins high up in some nests yesterday! Arrrooo! So well done our Flying Squad, good searching.

21

Now I will tell you a bit more about what wants solving.

KIDNAPS

The Case of the Small Missing Moose
The Case of the 3 Bunnies that Hopped it
The Case of the 4 Pinched Hedgepiglets
The Case of the Lost Lion Cub
The Case of the 4 Disappeared Ducklings, ect.

Also

ROBBINGS

The Case of the Jackdaw's Jewels
The Case of the Weasel's Gold Watch

SPOOKLY HAUNTINGS

The Case of the Green Bubble that Floats in the Night-time

Oo-er! What is happening? Where have the small brute beasts all gone? Who pinched the jewels and the watch? What comes floating about in the night like a green bubble? Do not fear and fret, do not get wurrid, the YFDA will soon find out. Arrrroooo!

Yours yellow-eyedly,

PS Mum always says yellow eyes are friends with the dark, yes? So look out clues, we are after you even with all the lights out.

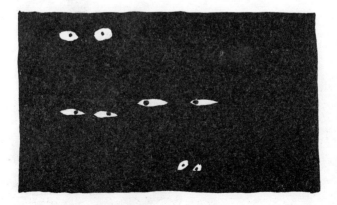

23

Sulking corner

Dear Mum and Dad,

Thank you for your harsh letter saying we are not proper detectives but you know somebody who is.

You say this somebody is not called a detective, but a Private Investigator which is a lot more posh. And he told you magnifying glasses are rubbish. He has got all hi-tech tools for detecting and he is called Furlock Homes-Wolf. And he is faymuss because he solved *The Hard Case of the Slippery Chicks*.

Now I feel all jealous.

Yours unpraisedly,

L Wolf

My desk (tidy 1 with all sharp pencils pointing same way)

Dear Mum and Dad,

Very busy work today using brute instinct and beastly senses. Today I will copy out some pages from our notebooks so you can say, hmm, nice detecting you cubs.

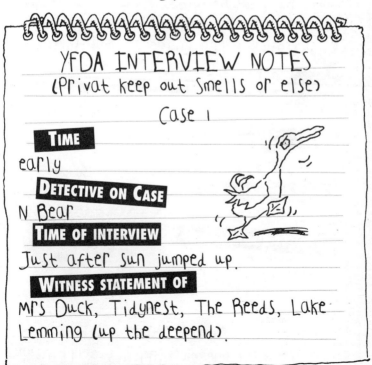

YFDA INTERVIEW NOTES
(Privat keep out Smells or else)

Case 1

TIME
early

DETECTIVE ON CASE
N Bear

TIME OF INTERVIEW
Just after sun jumped up.

WITNESS STATEMENT OF
Mrs Duck, Tidynest, The Reeds, Lake Lemming (up the deepend).

"I was bobbing up and down counting my babies like you do. I never seen feather nor beak of nobody, only that nice gingery man with a mask on his face and a sort of fur badge on his front. He was holding a bag of crumbs. Then I noticed all my fluffies was gorn. Gorn! Oh woe is me, ect."

PLAN

Normus will go hunting, in Lake Lemming area, for gingery man with mask on (bit suspish) plus furry badge also 4 small ducks with fluff on.

Case 2

DETECTIVE ON CASE

Yeller Wolf

TIME OF INTERVIEW

Just after snacktime

WITNESS STATEMENT OF

Mr and Mrs Lion,
Anywhere we feel like, Parching Plain.

"A travelling knifegrrrinder with squinty eyes came pushing his grrrrinder

over our hunting grrround. We noticed
he was wearing a fur brrrrooch and he
smelled minty. He said he had a special
offer on claw sharrrpening, so we
thought why not? It was just after he
went that we noticed our small cub was
not asleep in his patch of long grrrrass.
We rrrreckon he was cubnapped."

PLAN

Yeller to Parching Plain to track
suspect pushing minty knifegrinder with
fur brooch. Also looking for kidnapped
cub called Pounce (left ear chewed)

Case 3

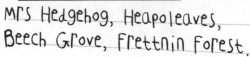

DETECTIVE ON CASE

S Crow

TIME OF INTERVIEW

Ark past 2

WITNESS STATEMENT OF

Mrs Hedgehog, Heapoleaves,
Beech Grove, Frettnin Forest.

"A gingery gypsy it was. Selling clothes
pegs with big spots. On her hanky.

She had a spotty hanky, you understand, see? Her clothes pegs were not spotty, right? I noticed she smelled minty and she had a fur thingy pinned to her blouse. Is that a help?

Snuffle snuffle. Excuse me. I am upset. I am always telling my hogglets never to take slugs from a stranger! But it was just too tempting for my little cheeky chestnuts. Now they have been torn from me. You must find them for me Mister Defective. I will pay anything. Slugs snails worms, you name it."

PLAN

Flying Squad (Stubbs) to do Air Search for suspect with special GO CROW! message on flying helmet.

Case 4

Co-Cheef Tec's Case (v hard, needs xtra keen beastly powers by me, hem hem)

PLAN

To detect who robbed the jewels plus the gold watch off the jackdaw and the weasel. My keen beastly ears, eyes, nose ect. tell me that jackdaw and weasel are making up fibs, just so I will find rich things for them. They hope I will say, "Da-daaah! Look at this shiny stuff I have found, are they yours by any chance, hem hem?" So then they can pretend, saying, "Oh defny, lovely, yes those are my treasures."

Yours R U kiddingly,

Your Little
Tracker

Dear Mum and Dad,

I know you like a good fib, so look at these woppers I wrote down in my notebook by shortpaw (quck wrtin):

Me (detectively): Tll me Mistr Jckdaw, whr did you hde yr jewels? Ws it in a gd hidy-hole?

Jackdaw (harshly): I tuckd ma sprkly jools nder a lmp of moss, see, and ma nest is way up top of a bell twer. So no way could any nrmal brute find it. It was a spook, I reckn.

Me (crafty): No nrmal brute, hem hem, I see. A spook, eh? Now let me ask Mr Weasel, dd you like yr gld wtch? Also, did you keep it in a daft place like on your frnt doorstp?

Weasel (front toothly): My gld watch was my best thing. It was worth a frtune. I kept it lockd in a chest hid at the btm of a deep dark tunl that I dug for it spesh. No brute knew where it was, only me. It must have been stln by a soopnachrel fors. By the way can you spell s-u-p-e-r-n-a-t-u-r-a-l f-o-r-c-e?

Me (correctingly): Oh, thanks. Now I cn spell it. But what Xactly is a supernatural force, hint hint?

Weasel: It is 1 of those nsty little green things that I saw come creepn into my bdrm in the drk on the bong of midnit. It was shockn. Would you like a description?

Me: Will I have to take it to the chemist?

Weasel: I said a DEscription not a PREscription.

Me: Thank you wunce morely.

Description of "not normal brute", "spook" and "nasty thing".

Small green Slimy- lot like a bat or a rat maybe

Can get up high bell towers, down secret tunnels, also into locked chests

floats pst noses

glowy and ghosty

Yours pulltheotheronely,

Little

My mat with all Supercub pics on

Dear Mum and Dad,

You say stop doing that silly short writing. Also you say my letter made you think of Uncle Bigbad and go all sad and snappish. But listen, why does that supernatural force remind you of Uncle? True, Uncle was a ghost and did glowing in the dark. But he was not 1 bit like the small ratty thing that the weasel saw floating by his nose in the night time. Uncle was a great big tall horrible ghost when he went haunting. He had a great big horrible furry face, plus big horrible red eyes, plus big horrible yellow teeth and all dribble dribbling down. Also his eyebrows met in the middle like Dad's only more caterpillary.

33

I know Uncle Bigbad got stolen in his whisky bottle from my house, but serves him right. He should not have scoffed so many bakebeans then he would not have died of the jumping beanbangs in the first place. And why didn't he stay in the nice grave I dug for him? He would have been safe there. He only moved into that bottle to show off, just because the label had 'Powerful Spirit' on it. Then he got corked up and spooknapped by Mister Twister the fox.

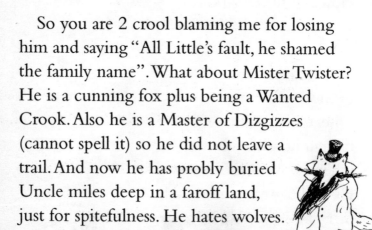

So you are 2 crool blaming me for losing him and saying "All Little's fault, he shamed the family name". What about Mister Twister? He is a cunning fox plus being a Wanted Crook. Also he is a Master of Dizgizzes (cannot spell it) so he did not leave a trail. And now he has probly buried Uncle miles deep in a faroff land, just for spitefulness. He hates wolves.

Yours suggestingly,

LB Wolf (helpful son)

Sock drawer

Dear Mum and Dad,

Your Spesh Delivery arrived today, so I got your tape recording of Dad having a fierce go at me. It was very scary, even listening in my sock drawer. I played it 2 times because 1st time I had socks stuffed 2 far up my ears.

So yes, alright, I am repeating after you,

1) I am a rubbish detective and not modern enuff.
2) It is a good idea if you want to send Private Investigator Furlock Homes-Wolf.
3) Yes, I understand. He is going to do some proper investigating and find all the lost small brutes and treasure quick.

4) Also, he will do hi-tech investigating about Uncle Bigbad and bring him back to Frettnin Forest so he can be a proud haunter wunce more and keep up the fierce name of Wolf in Beastshire.

Plus Smells is coming on the train with him and I must be a nice big bruv to him and not put him on a lead or in a kennel or anything.

Yours sighingly,

Little

Dear Mum and Dad,

Yesterday I had to go all the way south to Badpenny Junction to meet Furlock Homes-Wolf and Smells. It was a long trot by myself round Lake Lemming and across Shocking Marshes so I was a bit late.

Yeller, Stubbs and Normus are still out looking for missing small brutes. 3 more went missing in the night: 1 otter pup, 1 small squirrel plus 1 earwiggle. Also more brute beasts came in to say they saw the small floaty green glowmouse thing in the night. And when they woke up, their treasure was robbed. But no pawprints or anything.

When I got to the station I thought blow, missed them, because the train was going away puffingly in the distance. But no, a big, fat wolf was standing there on the platform. In 1 front paw he was holding a small hard suitcase, plus Smell's ted was in the other.

What flat feet he has got! Not mentioning
what a big hat and cape plus what big glasses!
I said, "Hello you must be Mister Furlock
Homes-Wolf. I am L Wolf,
Esqwire, Number 1 cub of
Gripper. Also, Co-Cheef
Detective of the YFDA."

He said, "Did
somebody speak?"

I said, "Yes, me
down here under your
big tummy."

He said, "I knew that
actually. Wait there while I work out who you
are on my hi-tech laptop machine." Then he
opened the suitcase and went clickerty click,
keypad keypad keypad. Then he said, "Ah,
elementary my dear Spotson, you must be
Master... er... Knitting Wool."

I said, "No, I am Little Wolf" and he said,
"I knew that actually. The machine is never
wrong."

I said, "Excuse me, where is my baby bruv and why are you holding his ted's paw?"

He said, "Ted? Don't be ridiculous. Ted is on the luggage rack with my suitcase. See for yourself."

I said, "But Mister Furlock, the train left five mins ago" and he said, "I just said that actually!"

Never mind, I spect Smells will turn up in Lost Property tomorrow.

Yours tufflucky (only kidding),

Little

Dear Mum and Dad,

Me and Mister Furlock Homes-Wolf had to go all the way down to Nasty Bend today to fetch Smells from the Lost Property office there. The guardman made me pay a big fine for Smells because of him doing monkey swings on the emerjuncy string. Also pretending to be luggage (plus eating the station master's wissul).

Smells went whiny and would not walk so I had to piggyback him all the way home with the hic-wissuls. Also, I had to keep picking up Mister Furlock. He trips over a lot. (He is ~~shortsitid~~, ~~shirtseated~~, needs thick gogs).

Yeller, Normus and Stubbs were waiting for us at the YFDA, but all a bit gloomish because of not solving *any* cases or finding *any* lost small brutes.

Mister Furlock said, "Aha! That is because of you not being hi-tech. Tomorrow I shall show you sad small dim detectives some *proper* investigating." Then he ate all the supper and got his head stuck in the stewpot.

Your peckish cub,

Little Starver

Dear Mum and Dad,

Mister Homes-Wolf says we may call him Furlock now, plus he let us have a look at his special investigator power-tools.

Here is a pic to show small detectives why using your keen beastly senses is rubbish.

Technotracker™ – featuring:

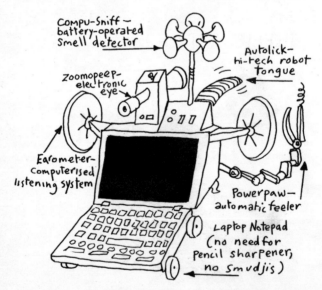

Compu-Sniff – battery-operated smell detector

Autolick – hi-tech robot tongue

Zoomopeep – electronic eye

Earometer – computerised listening system

Powerpaw – automatic feeler

Laptop Notepad (no need for pencil sharpener, no smudjis)

Plus it shows Y using your animal instincts is much 2 old fash.

Furlock gave us a lesson on how to do automatic sniffing at dinner time. He went clickerty click keypad keypad keypad.

Then the machine said (robot voice), "Nasal report! You have a fine cheese on the table. Smellymentary my dear Watson."

Yeller said, "SORRY TO MENTION IT, BUT MY NOSE REPORTS THERE IS NO CHEESE ON THE TABLE, JUST YOUR FEET MISTER FURLOCK!"

Furlock said, "I knew that actually. The keys are a little sticky, that's all."

Furlock says he will do more lessons tomorrow if I pay him 3 gold coins. Handy, because that is just how many Stubbs found in Frettnin Forest the other day. Arrrooo!

Yours Xpectingalottly,

Little

Dear Mum and Dad,

Our lesson today was looking for Furlock's
lost glasses. We spent 3 hours looking for
them with the Technotracker. It found 1
window, some marbles, 2 jamjars and the
bathroom mirror. Then Smells went har har,
he had them on all the time. He
likes wearing them, he says
they make him go all funny
and giddy.

Furlock said, "I knew that actually. Now, I
think you cubs would learn a lot if I told you
how I solved my most *celebrated* case, *The
Case of the Slippery Chicks*.
Are you familiar with it?"

Normus said, "Not
really, you have only
told us it 15 times."

45

So Furlock said good, and he told us again.

It was wunce upon a cold early spring-time. All the wolves up the hilly end of Lonesome Woods (near your lair) were starving hungry, so they prowled round looking for some tasty snacks to pounce on. Then along came a chicken with 7 chicks. But the wolves could not catch hold of the chicks to eat, they were much 2 slippery (so shaming). So they called for Mister Furlock Holmes-Wolf, Investigator, hem hem. Then off he went crawlingly through the frosty grass and soonly he came up to a chicken's nest. He pointed his machine at it. And guess what the Technotracker detected? The hen with a butterknife in her beak, spreading margarine on her babies. So he pinched her butterknife. And that was how he became a Faymuss Wolf Hero and Hi-tech Investigator. The end.

Normus did a whisper to me saying, "Hum, I could have spied that hen in just 3 secs, I bet." But Furlock said paws on lips, no talking. Then he told us about some other faymuss cases he solved. *The Case of the Polished Piggies, The Case of the Hairoiled Hares, The Case of the Soapy Snakes, The Case of the Hard to Hold Eels*, plus *The Case of the Skiddy Sausage Dogs*, ect. So boring.

Stubbs said, "Ark! Arkzactly" meaning aren't these cases arkzactly the same?" Yeller said, "YEAH, AREN'T THEY KIND OF... IDENTICAL?"

That was when we all got donked on the head with the Technotracker.

Yours bumply,

L Wolf.

PS Ouch.

Dear Mum and Dad,

Furlock said I could have a go with the Technotracker if I gave him xtra Moosepops at snacktime. He said, "Anyway, you had better test it out in case you damaged it with your heads yesterday."

So I went clickerty click, keypad keypad keypad and the machine said: "Hearing alert! A small mouse just crept in. It scoffed all the Moosepops and removed the turnups from Investigator Furlock's trousers."

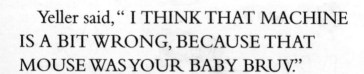

Yeller said, " I THINK THAT MACHINE IS A BIT WRONG, BECAUSE THAT MOUSE WAS YOUR BABY BRUV."

Normus said, "Hum, have another go."

So I went clickerty click, keypad keypad keypad and the machine went, "Nasal alert! The house is on fire."

Stubbs went, "Ark! Smark" meaning Yes, I smell smark as well!

But not really, because guess what? Stubbs put furballs in Furlock's pipe, to make a cosy nest!

Yours coffingly,

L

PS I think the Technotracker is a bit rubbish. The YFDA are better clue hunters (true).

By the big window, staring out (Xcitedly)

Dear Mum and Dad,

Guess what? We had a circus come from Murkshire today. But then all the animals got kidnapped so no show, boo shame. I wanted to see the helifant in case it looks like a helicopter (I like flying).

I am still hopeless at hi-tech work but here is some GOOD NEWS! You know that small moose that went missing? Stubbs found out he has come back to his herd. Arrroooo! Funny thing is, his antlers. They have gone all rubbery so not much good for butting with. Oo-er.

Yours Yzatly?

Little ??????

Dear Mum and Dad,

More good news! All the small lost brutes have been unkidnapped, not just the snacky 1s but the fierce pouncers also.

They all said the same kind of story, like this. A nice gingery gypsy or minty sweep or knifegrinder came up to them and looked into their eyes saying, softly, softly: "My boys, you must come to my lovely dark den with me." So they went far off from Frettnin Forest.

Then they got put in cages. Then they had to be partners with 1 other small brute and go into a nice big metal room. Next they had to hold paws and do Ringa Ringa Rosie.

Plus funny sparks started shooting about. Then they all fell down. Then they could not remember. Then they came back to Frettnin Forest to live happy ever after (a tickoff by their mums and dads for talking to strangers).

Only they are not xactly the same as before. Like the ducklings. If their mum drops a plate and it goes BANG!! all the ducklings come quacking up quick saying, "Hello, we like bangs". Also the hedgehogglet has got a zip under his tummy, so now he can take off his prickles, easy cheesy. All the little rabbits say, "Maa-aa" and won't hide down their holes. Plus they want their mum to knit them white woolly jumpers.

This is funny 2. The lion cub has gone off meat, all he wants is toffee apples.

This looks like a job for THE YFDA! Arrrooo! We are soooooo xcited!

Yours petitly,

Hercule Poireau   (french tec)

PS Moi really.

Dear Mum and Dad,

No, I won't let *your* darling baby pet go off on his own with any knifegrinder or minty stranger. But tell him not to be such a ~~noosence noosense~~ pain. He keeps flashing the torch from our detective kit plus handcuffing the Technotracker.

Your niggly,

Senior Boy (hem hem)

Dear Mum and Dad,

Da-daah! We have a new case!

A hermit came knocking at our door today saying, "Good day, I would like to speak to a detective."

I was just going to say, "Hello, I am Little Wolf, Co-Cheef Detective," but Furlock said buttinnly, "You are fortunate. Please enter. Allow me to introduce myself. Furlock Holmes-Wolf, celebrated Hi-Tech Investigator at your service."

The hermit came in with a wopping cloak on. He had sharp eyes, big boots plus rubber gloves. Also he smelled of catmint and his trousers were all bunchy at the back. He said (hermitly), "Good morrow. I am a just a poor old hermit. I live in a woodcutter's cottage by

55

myself and last night I was visited by a horrid green spookly thing. I have nothing to rob, but I fear I shall be kidnapped. I need protecting. Is that part of your YFDA service?"

Furlock said, "Fear no more, old hermit. 3 of my young helpers, Yeller, Normus and Smellybreff will protect you. I personally shall bring my faithful Technotracker to investigate the green intruder."

Yeller said, "GOOD, I LIKE PROTECTIN."

Normus said, "Yes, and I like bashing intruders."

I said, "Hey, do not forget me and Stubbs?"

So Furlock said, "Little Wolf and Stubby Crow will remain here in case of emergencies."

Then Smells started whining, saying he was not going, he hated woodcutters' huts. But then the hermit's sharp eyes went wide and he said softly, "My boy, something tells me that you are a keen young chappie who is eager to assist an old hermit in his difficulties." Smells did not know how to say no to him. So off they *all* went in a small keen pack.

Oh boo, I hate staying at home, not fair.

Yours fedduply,

Littly

Dear Mum and Dad,

Me and Stubbs waited and waited all night
but no emerjuncies for us, boo shame.

At sunjump we wanted to be busy so we ran
rushingly on the trail with our magnifying
glasses. We followed the boot and
pawprints for many a minute

and many an hour
because it went all zigzaggy. But that
did not put us off, because after long searching
in the deep dark forest we found the woodcutter's hut in a clearing. It was just on the
north edge of Frettnin Forest,

(you could see Windy Ridge behind). In we
went boldly, but – oh no! it was all empty. We
looked round sadly, then out came my detective
kit notebook and sharp pencil. I stuck on my
Clues sticker and did this writing:

CLUES

- 1 big room, few books, big fireplace, not much ~~fernichure funnychif~~ chairs ect.
- loads of rope (v sticky)
- 1 Technotracker — bashed to bits on floor
- 1 screwed up piece of paper (nothing on it)
- large rubber gloves
- loads of dandylion stalks with seeds blown off
- 1 of these ——>

Then we went hurryingly outside again to look for a new trail. Stubbs did Air Searching but we could only find the trail we came by, not 1 other whiff or print! Where has everybody gone?

Yours scratchheadly,
   Little ????

Dear Mum and Dad,

Now the Technotracker is dead, me and Stubbs must do our detecting the good old fash way (loads of brute instinct, plus use keen beastly senses, ect. remember?).

So Stubbs unscrewed the paper. He made it nice and flat and laid it on the floor but no writing on it.

Next he started poking his clever beak into the books while I had a good sniff and lick round the room, thinking, Hmmm, all that funny rope. Y is it so thick and sticky? What is that metal thing called a HE? Y are there no fingerprints of the hermit, because I can see loads of pawprints of Furlock, Yeller, Normus and Smells?

Also I could smell all the different smells of them, plus a strong scent of catmint. I said outloudly, "Hmm, catmint, let me see..." and all of a suddenly, Stubbs said, "Ark!" meaning look what I have found in the enzarkclopedia!

He showed me how somebody had turned down the corner of 1 page, at letter C for... **catmint**. Quick as a chick, I read the words on the page:

> **Catmint: A fine smelly plant loved by cats and other cunning pouncers. The smell is strong enough to cover up all kinds of other strong scents, including parsley, mint, rosemary, thyme and** Pepper

And guess what? On the word *pepper* there was a pawprint. "That is a foxprint!" I xclaimed. Stubbs went, "Ark!" meaning arkstraordinary detecting work.

And which fox would go "Pepper! Yessss!"
And poke the word with his paw? Stubbs
went, "Ark" meaning it is arksactly the same
fox who would dress up as a gypsy, knifegrinder or hermit.

Answer: **Mister Twister!**

Smellymintery my dear parentals!

 LW

PS But which way did he go?

The Fireplace, Woodcutter's Cottage, Frettnin Forest

Dear Mum and Dad,

2 branes are better than 1, that is Y me and Stubbs are good workouters.

Stubbs went to have a good look up the chimney so I had a close look at the funny metal thing with HE on. It had a little tap on it. I gave it a turn and it went FSSSSSSHH! So scary!

But now in my notebook I write…

SOLVED MYSTERIES

Who was that hermit?
Answer, Mister Twister, cunning fox and master of Dizgizzes (cannot spell it) ✓

Y did he have bunchy trousers at the back?
Answer, to hide his bushy red tail ✓

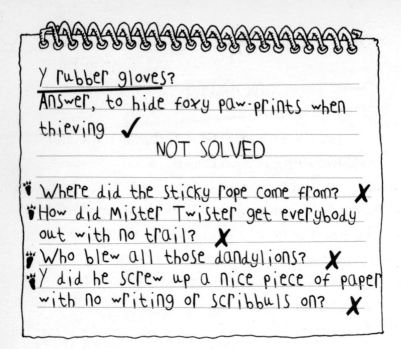

Y rubber gloves?

Answer, to hide foxy paw-prints when thieving ✓

NOT SOLVED

🐾 Where did the sticky rope come from? ✗

🐾 How did Mister Twister get everybody out with no trail? ✗

🐾 Who blew all those dandylions? ✗

🐾 Y did he screw up a nice piece of paper with no writing or scribbuls on? ✗

Wait. Stubbs has come back down the chimney saying "Ark!" meaning he is all arkscited. Must find out Y. Will write again soonly.

Yours investigately,

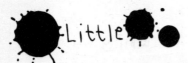

Little

PS Do you know an investigator is an alligator in a vest (not really, joke to stop you going sob, where is our baby?)

Dear Mum and Dad,

Good thing Stubbs got
nice and sooty
because he landed
on that unscrewed
piece of paper
and had a good
shake. It was
like a magic
thing because
letters came
up on the
paper! I will
say Y. Because
of someone
(being Mister
Twister) using it to
lean on when he was
doing heavy writing on
another piece of paper on
top. Get it? He made all dents and lines and
when they got sooty they looked like this:

**The Hermitage, Woodcutter's Cottage,
The Clearing, Frettnin Forest, Beastshire**

My Dear Bookseller,

I like reading a great deal. Rush me the
following books that interest me strangely.

**EXPERIMENTING WITH ANIMALS
by Ken U. Altrum
MUCKING ABOUT WITH GENES
by I. M. Rich
HOW TO BUILD YOUR OWN GENETIC
MODIFICATION CHAMBER
by Ivor Startupp-Kitt**

Yours urgently,

A. Hermit

Stubbs went, "Arks" meaning
arkstraordinary, is that how you spell 'jeans'?
But we found *Genetic Modification* in the

enzarklopedia. It said it means changing
things by messing about with their insides.
That is a bit 2 hard for us, we are only small.
So *what* is that cunning fox up to?

But now, clever Stubbs has detected how
Mister Twister got away. I will say later but
Stubbs is saying "Ark!" meaning arkscuse
him. He wants me to help him quick. He is
making something with his clever beak. It is
good.

Yours bizzybeely,

Buzzy

Dear Mum and Dad,

What do you think? I am sending you this nice pic of our airship we made in the night-time. We made it out of the sticky rope, the wastepaper basket and a rubber glove blown up with FSSSSSSSSH out of the metal thing with HE on. (If you turn it round it has got LIUM on its back. HE + LIUM = gas for blowing up balloons and airships! We looked that up in the enzarklopedia big book too!)
Arrrooo!

Now I 'spect you will say, Little Wolf, what are you up 2 now? Answer, flying north-north-eastly on the trail of Mister Twister. But you will say, Little, do not be such a guesser. How can you tell Mister Twister went away airly? Also how can you tell which way he went?

Answer, *helium-entary* my dear Mum and Dad! Because:

1) Stubbs has done big Air Searches lately, meaning he knows the wind here is a north–north–east 1.

2) He found loads of pawprints going just 1 way.

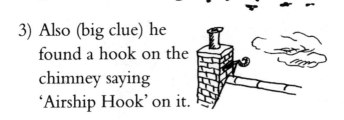

3) Also (big clue) he found a hook on the chimney saying 'Airship Hook' on it.

4) He found loads more dandylions with the seeds blown off. That was a hard puzzle but we did a shut-your-eyes-and-think-squeezingly. All of a suddenly, Stubbs said, "Ark!" meaning eurarka, I have found out something!

I said, "What?" Answer. Mister Twister was
holding up dandylion clocks to find out *how*
strong the wind was blowing and *which way*!
So well done our Flying Squad!

Your breezy boy,

L W

PS Hmm, flying.
Lovely.

Dear Mum and Dad,

We have landed bonkingly near Broken Tooth Caves. Stubbs wanted to let all the FSSSSSH out with a sharp peck. But I said no, save it for later. So we hid the airship behind a big rock. Now it is v dark, but Stubbs is holding the torch in his clever beak so I can do my writing. A good job we had our detective kit with us.

The paths round here are rocky, so no pawprints, but we found 1 good clue:

This is a button off Smells's sailor suit, so he is probably kidnapped and in a cave. With the others, I bet. BUT (big but) which cave? There are many!

It is creepy here. My beastly instinct has gone all tickly like when I see a big hairy spider. There must be lots of spiders very close by.

Oooooooooooooooooooooo°!

What was that? A loud trumpet noise! Sorry about smudje. All quiet now. We are starving. Wish I had 1 of Mum's rabbit rolls or a tasty mice pie yum yum. I will have to look for emerjuncy rations instead.

Yours rummagingly,

Littly

Dear Mum and Dad,

Did I say we were both starving hungry and wishing for Mum's rabbit rolls yum yum? Well I got out my emerjuncy matchbox to see if I had any tasty crawlers in it for crunchy snacks. It was empty, boo shame. So out with our magnifying glasses and off we went searchingly in the crooks and nannies. (Other way round, sorry.)

We searched and searched. My yellow eyes made friends with the dark but then

HELP!
TYRANOSAURUS
REX!

Yours hoppitly,

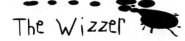

The Wizzer

Dear Mum and Dad,

You want to go careful with magnifying glasses. Sometimes they do tricks to trick you, because you know that T-rex? It was a stick insect really. The magnifying glass was just pretending.

Never mind because, guess what? The stick insect jumped in my match box. So handy! I was just going to give it a nibble but Stubbs said, "Ark", meaning that is arkstraordinary! Y did the stick insect just hop in your matchbarks like that?

So I said, "Tell me, Mister Crunchy Snack, how did you learn to do hopping so high?" And the insect said (stickly), "I learned it off of a cricket. I had to hold hands with him and do a Ringa Ringa Rosie in the metal room that went all sparky."

I said, "Oo-er, I have heard that Ringa Ringa Rosie story before. Were you by any chance captured by a foxy hermit? Or a minty knifegrinder? Or a gingery gypsy?"

The sticky said back, "Yes I was! But I…" Stubbs said, "Ark!" meaning, you arkscaped.

The sticky said, "Cor what a clever cub and crowchick you are. You should be detectives."

I said a proud aha. "Aha we *are* detectives. We are from the YFDA. And that foxy kidnapper was none other than Mister Twister, master of dizzgizzes (cannot spell it) and wanted crook of Frettnin Forest. Now tell us what happened because I am always ready, and my pencil is a sharp 1."

Yours notingly,

L

Dear Mum and Dad,

We have made friends with Sticky, he is nice and a good watcher so no eating him. (Lucky Stubbs shared his wiggly grubs with me, so my tummy is not 2 rumbly now.)   Sticky says he has seen lots of cages here. They are full of captured brute beasts, some big, some small. All sorts. The biggest 1 is grey, like a big wrinkly house with 4 legs. It has ears like car doors, plus a hosepipe in the front for tunes and hoovering you up. Praps that is the helifant that got kidnapped from the circus. Praps it was him made us jump with his loud trumpet.

Also, Sticky says, sometimes Mister Twister carries a whisky bottle. He holds it up like a lantern when he goes walking in the dark tunnels and looking in the cages. He says it shines with a green glow. Oh no, I think that green glowness is the ghost of Uncle Bigbad! So shaming to end up as a lamp for a fox!

1 other bad thing is, Mister Twister has got 2 terrible creatures to guard the cages all the time. They are big as cats and fierce with 8 furry legs like spiders! They made all that sticky rope, I bet! No wonder my fur feels tickly all the time. Spiders are my worst thing ('cept for loud bangs).

Sticky told us that the last things Mister Twister captured were 4 cocoons, like silkworms. 1 was a big, fat cocoon. Another was big and furry. 1 was small and loud. Then there was a small 1 with a sailor hat on. That is Furlock, Normus, Yeller and Smells I bet. Captured by the hermit. Sticky says they are locked up in the Hall of Cages, near the metal room that goes sparky, and guarded by spidercat guards.

Sticky wants to come rescuing with us. He wants to save his chum the cricket. Because he cannot jump away himself. Good eh?

Stubbs said, "Ark!" meaning do not worry, we will help the crarket to arkscape!

Pawscrossly for luck,

 Little cheef

Dear Mum and Dad,

We are in Broken Tooth Caves. It is drippy and ploppy and so much tunnels. But Sticky has good feelers for finding the way in the darkness. We must not use Stubby's torch, 2 giveaway, so I am writing this in glowworm juice. Hope U can read it.

Wait. We have found the Hall of Cages. It is quiet. We can hear small snores. That is a mouse snore. That is a badger. A ferret, a squirrel. Tippy on the toes. Wait. My nose is telling me. Yes! I smell a baby bruv. He is near. I must use my keenly senses. Wish my yellow eyes were *more* keen.

Ooo-er! There is Smells in his little cocoon –
very still, no wiggling! Also Yeller, Normus
and Furlock all stuck up tight. And such a big
lock on the cage door.

Oh no, help! Stubbs has got pounced on!

Yours panickly,

Dear Mum and Dad,

It was Mister Twister's Spidercat
Guards! Huge miaowing spiders – help!
They came swinging from the roof on
their sticky ropes. Stubbs gave 1 a hard peck but
they were 2 strong and tied him up spinningly.

Up went my fur, all tickly on my back. That
was my beastly instinct saying 2 me, *Look out
behind you, Little!* I went flat but then Stubbs
called "Ark!" meaning fire arkstinguisher! It
was just by me on the wall.

Bang I went on the button and out came
the water with a SHUSHHHHH! Har har,
that was a good hard skwirter. I shouted, "Put
your legs up, you Spidercats! I am a proud

detective wolf, so you are under arrest. Give
me the keys to the cages."
They tried to pounce
on me swiftly. So I
skwirted and
skwirted them
right in the nasty
eyes and right in
the nasty teeth. I
chased them along the
Hall of Cages till they came
to a big drainhole and DOWN they went
wooshingly. And guess

what? The keys
dropped out of
their horrible
mouths!

Yours servumrightly,

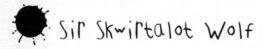

Sir Skwirtalot Wolf

Dear Mum and Dad,

I got the penknife out of my Detective Kit and cut Stubbs free. Then we unlocked the cage and Stubbs got busy with his clever beak. All the sticky rope was in heaps on the floor before you could say a kwick thing like, "Hello everybody, we have come to save you".

Yeller said, "WELL DONE LITTLE AND STUBBS." But Smells gave me a sharp nip because he likes being tied up. And Furlock said, "I knew you would come actually. Did you find us by my Technotracker?"

I said, "No we found you by our eyes, noses and other beastly senses, because we are the YFDA. And the Technotracker is defnly a TechNOtracker now. It was Mister Twister who did smashing up."

He said, "What? Did you say *smashing up*? TSO! TSO! Quick!"

Normus said, "What is TSO — is it bashing?"

Furlock said, "TSO is Trot Swiftly Off! NOW!"

I said, "But we have nearly found out WHODUNNIT and WOTFOR. And we have to rescue Uncle Bigbad's ghost. And what about freeing the other brute beasts and arresting Mister Twister?"

Furlock said, "Frankly, I do not care a flea WHODUNNIT or WOTFOR, or for Bigbad Wolf either. He is far too wild for my liking. I intend to TSO before anyone thinks of smashing *me* up. If you have any sense, you will join me while you still can. Goodbye. Whoops." And off he rushed, trippingly. He was only wurrid about saving himself. Oh blow.

Yours leftinthelurchly,

THE YFDA

Dear Mum and Dad,

Pity about Furlock, eh? Ask Dad to give him a good nip next time he sees him.

Yeller said, "GOOD RIDDANCE TO HIM! AND WELL DONE, CHUMS! YOU SAVED US. THAT CRAFTY FOX WAS GOIN TO EXPERIMENT ON US TODAY. HE WAS GOIN TO PUT US IN HIS METAL ROOM. HE SAID WE ARE THE LAST PART OF HIS CUNNIN PLAN."

Normus said, "Yes, well done fellers! Now we can do some bashing at last!"

I said, "No bashing yet, Normus. 1st we must find out Mister Twister's cunning plan. Where is he?"

Yeller said, "HE IS IN A LOCKED ROOM TALKIN INTO HIS TAPE RECORDER."

I said, "Then we must use our keenly senses to find out what he is saying."

Normus said, "Shame we haven't got an electronic listening device like Furlock had. We could bug the room with that."

That made Yeller have 1 of his Big Ideers. He said, "BUG-AMENTARY MY DEAR NORMUS! WE **WILL** PUT A BUG INTO LISTEN. BUT NO NEED FOR ELECTRIC!"

Sticky said bravely, "I'm a bug. Will I do?" but Stubbs said, "Ark!" meaning, what about your friend the crarket? He would be even better.

Time for Hunt the Cricket. Arrroooo!

Yours eagerly,

 The YFDA

Dear Mum and Dad,

It did not take long finding the cricket, he was in a jamjar close by. He was a bit wurrid in case of getting scoffed, but then he was happy to be a detective bug for us.

We went shushly along the dark Hall of Cages. Soonly we found a big strong door saying TOP SECRET– CRAFTY FOXES ONLY! Quick as a chick we popped the cricket in the keyhole, so he could see and hear that cunning crook and kidnapper Mister Twister. Plus he could talk to us, by rubbing his legs together chirpingly. Good eh?

Yours spyly,

 Little Eye

Dear Mum and Dad,

Here is the cricket news (translated by
Sticky, he speaks cricket best). This was
spoken softly into a tape recorder by Mister
Twister about his secret Xperiments!

**"Crafty Plan, Code Name PYOF.
Listening Diary of My Crafty Self, Day
43.** Testing, testing. Hello, dear boy. As I speak
today, my Master Plan is almost complete, so I
shall give myself the pleasure
of summing up my
remarkable achievement.
My first brilliant stroke
was to kidnap my rival
in crime, the once great
and terrible Bigbad Wolf.
The label on the whisky
bottle where he resides reads
'Powerful Spirit'. What nonsense that seems,
for now – ha ha – he is my pet, my slave. And
why must he do all that I command? Simple!

"The answer is pinned to my chest. It is a well known fact that he who dares to snatch a single hair from the tail of a wolf shall master him forever – and I have his entire *tail*! How? I hear you cry! By craft and cunning, for I knew that the wretch had blown himself to pieces as a result of eating bakebeans too fast. I also discovered that the only part of him that his pesky nephew, Little Wolf, could find to bury was his whiskers. So patiently I searched and snuffed, never giving up until I had tracked down the tail that has made my fortune!

"Knowing that ghosts can always find hidden stores of gold and jewels, my first command to him was to keep his miniature shape and size, and to do all my treasure seeking. That allowed me time to kidnap at least 1 small brute of every species in Frettnin Forest. And to study.

"Very soon I taught my sharp self the science of genetic modification, for I wished to change the kidnapped creatures for the *better*. Better for me, that is! My aim was to turn them into *convenience food*! Once Bigbad had stolen enough treasure to allow me to do so, I purchased a beautiful machine – my metal box – my Genetic Modification Chamber! After that, I began my Great Plan, **Code Name PYOF!** It has been a huge success and is almost complete. I am switching off now in order to carry our my final Master Stroke!"

Oh no, he is coming out.....

Yours hidingly,

Dear Mum and Dad,

Back we all went gaspingly to the Hall of Cages. Cricket's legs were stiff from so much chirping, but we all had to use our keenly beastly senses quick! This is our plan:

1) Sticky and Cricket – take keys and open up all the cages
2) Me and Stubbs – hide high up in the shadows
3) Normus, Yeller and Smells – pretend to be tied up again in their cage (Smells likes that part)
4) Get a big, fat sack so it looks like Furlock is in the cage 2.

I will tell you the rest if it works.

Yours riskingly,

 L Wolf

PS If not, goodbye forever, Mum and Dad. We tried our best. Call out the Murkshire Wolf Pack and get ready to have a fight against Mister Twister before he gets you 2.

Dear M and D,

Not dead, but nearly, phew. I will say what happened:

Up lit the hall with the green glow of Uncle Bigbad. Mister Twister was holding Uncle up by his bottle to light the way. He was speaking into his tape recorder again, saying softly:

"Listening Diary, Day 43, continued.
As I was saying before I interrupted myself, my Master Plan is to turn Frettnin Forest into a **PYOF** or **Pounce on Your Own Forest**! I shall soon be able to feast on all my favourite creatures with *no danger to myself whatsoever*! My prey will be easy and my enemies will be feeble and powerless against me! I shall grow gorgeously fat and sleek and never have a single worry.

"Using my GM chamber, I have mixed up the shapes and habits of my kidnap victims, large and small. Already I have created a vegetarian lion by crossing him with a baa-lamb. I have crossed a pheasant with a gun-dog, so that it runs towards hunters with shotguns. I have crossed a hedgehog with a washbag so that I can unzip his prickles and have a deliciously instant snack. A piggy has been crossed with a rabbit so that he will pop straight into the cooking pot, crying 'Lucky me, I have found my burrow!' A shy little mouse has been crossed with a hyena so now I can hear him laughing, no matter how tall the grass is where he hides.

He He He.

"One by one I am returning these changed creatures to their homes. Only yesterday I sent back a young squirrel. His mother is wondering why he is terrified of heights and will not climb up to his dray. She has no idea that I have crossed him with a mole!

"Now, as a special treat for myself, I have saved the best experiment till last. I intend to cross some meddling wolves and an interfering young bear with a litter of poodle pups. After just 30 seconds playing Ring-a-Ring-a-Roses in my GM Chamber, they will all be tamed. They will roll over on their backs and let me tickle their tummies! Spidercat guards bring out the prisoners!"

Help!

Yours tobecontinuedly,

The proud cubs
    of Frettnin Forest

Dear M and D,

Har har, hee hee, I love having my tummy tickled by a crafty fox (not really, only kidding).

We had a nice BIG shock for Mister Twister. Me and Stubbs were The Flying Squad. We came dropping quick out of the roof shadows. Down we whooshed swingingly on a sticky rope. I put out my paws like an X and Stubbs sat on my head and made an X with his legs and wings. So when Mister Twister saw our shadow coming, he thought we were a Spidercat guard!

Then Yeller gave his war howl – ARROOOOOOOOO! He and Normus

and Smells threw their ropes off, opened their cage and charged snappingly at the vain and peppery plotter. Mister Twister tried to bash them with his tape recorder, but I kept swinging and knocked him over with a flying kick. That was when Stubbs grabbed Uncle Bigbad's whisky bottle in his clever beak and flew away with it.

And guess what I got with my clever paw? Uncle's tail!

Sticky and Cricket were good unlockers. Out came all the kidnapped creatures chargingly. They butted and pecked and bashed and bit and gave that fox a good noisy fight. The helifant made his scariest trumpet noise and did a lot of nice squashing and squishing and swishing with his hosepipe. He was sooooo Xcited to be out of his cage!

But he lost his way in the darkness and got himself stuck in the GM Chamber, boo shame.

That made Mister Twister get his cunningness up again. He turned his foxy eyes on us saying, "Now my boys, stop all this roughness. Just look deep deeeep into my eyes and do what I command." Good thing my brute instinct called out to Stubbs,  "Quick! Throw the whisky bottle to the helifant." So he did a swift loop the loop. Then the helifant's hosepipe reached up and sucked the bottle out of his beak. I banged the door shut and switched the switch, click.

The Chamber started to shake and spark and rock as the helifant did Ringa Ringa Rosie with the ghost of Uncle Bigbad. Then

BLAM!

The Chamber door flew off and

Out came flying the faymuss Terror of Haunted Hall. It was the good old ghost of Uncle Bigbad, back to his normal monster size! He had his great big horrible red eyes and his great big horrible yellow teeth and all his horrible dribble dribbling down. Arrrooooo!

Yours victori-ussly,

The YFDA

PS I have done a nice pic of Mister Twister with a bashed up tail and lots of lumps running away limply.

Safely home again

Dear Mother and Father of mine
(posh, eh?),

I ~~reseaved~~ ~~receeved~~ ~~received~~ got your letter
saying Furlock came round to the Lair going
moan groan, no more hi-tech investigating
for him. He is opening a
sticking plaster shop for sad
wolves that keep tripping up
and bumping their knees.
And it is all my fault.

You say I am a bad boy because I did not
let Smells do handcuffing on Mister Twister,
he wanted to do that spesh. So now he is all
upset. Also you say I must spoil your darling
baby ~~pest~~ pet more, like letting him get
cubnapped and tied up more often because
those are his favourites. You say let him have
loads more ruff fun and give in to him all the
time, it is the only way.

Har har, I know that is just your wolfly way
to say well done, and pat pat for cunningness.

Also you mean to say congratarrooooshuns
for solving loads of tricky cases all in 1 go by
trying hard plus normal wolfly sense and
brute instinct. Plus doing all that rescuing and
saving Frettnin Forest from being a Pounce
on Your Own Forest for one fat fox.

You are sooo nice, hem hem joke.

Yours proud Co-Cheefly,

Moi (French)

My office, a long time later

Dear Mum and Dad,

Since my last letter, The YFDA has done a lot of genetic unmodification on the kidnapped brute beasts that got put in the Chamber. Because we want Frettnin Forest back to its normal wild self. Also we wanted Uncle to go back to his proper happy haunting ground and keep up the terrible name of Wolf. Arrroooo! (I have given him back his tail but, guess what? Ssshhh, I kept 1 small hair, just in case I need to boss him about. Because then if me, Yeller and Normus want to be pirates or spacecubs, he might come in handy, yesss?)

Your busy boy,

L. Wolf
Co-Cheef Detective YFDA

No, Mum and Dad, I do not mean be like peabugs. This is your invitaysh to come and see our mini circus, it is a BIG THRILL!

I have done you a pic of SMELLYBREFF
THE CLOWN doing a skwirt with his
HELIFANTEDDY. He made the helifant do
Ringa Ringa Rosie with his ted, before we
put wheels on the GM Chamber and turned
it into a nice caravan, cosy hmmmm.

Sticky and Cricket wanted to stay being
modified, so now they can be THE
AMAZING JUMPING TINY T-REX and
HIS FRIEND THE CRICKET ON STILTS.

The helifant likes being shrunk best 2.
Good because he is a nice attraction.
He can play his trumpet and
also be THE WORLD'S
ONLY HELIFANT IN
A BOTTLE.

Also we have got THE
WORLD'S LOUDEST RING
MASTER YELLER WOLF!
And Normus is our
STRONGEST
BEARCUB EVER!

Me and Stubbs are trapezers called THE FLYING SPIDERCATS.

We are brill, come and have a thrill.

Yours swingingly,

Little Bigtop

ARROOOOOOOOO!!!

Little Wolf's Book of Badness

Ian Whybrow, illustrated by Tony Ross

All Little Wolf wants to do is stay at home with Mum, Dad and baby brother Smellybreff. Instead, he is packed off to Cunning College to learn the 9 Rules of Badness and earn a Gold BAD Badge from his wicked Uncle Bigbad. He sets off on his journey, sending letters home as he adventures in the big bad world.

'Little Wolf ranks among the most engaging animal characters in modern children's writing.' *She*

ISBN 0 00 675160 1

Collins

An imprint of HarperCollins*Publishers*

Little Wolf's Diary of Daring Deeds

Ian Whybrow, illustrated by Tony Ross

Little Wolf and his cousin Yeller decide that BADNESS is out, and ADVENTURES are in. But their first mistake is thinking that they can buy adventures. Their second mistake is to reply to Mister Marvo's advert for Instant Adventures (Scary but Safe). The result is that they find themselves caught up in a *real* adventure. But Little is scared of bangs; snow gives Yeller the trembles; their new friend Stubbs, the crow, is too frit to fly and… Smellybreff gets cubnapped!

'A howlingly funny book for all the family to get their teeth into.' *Young Telegraph*

ISBN 0 00 675252 7

An imprint of HarperCollinsPublishers

Little Wolf's Haunted Hall for Small Horrors

Ian Whybrow, illustrated by Tony Ross

Little Wolf and Yeller start up a new scary school for brute beasts. Their lessons include Hunting for Gold in the daytime, plus Horror Haunting at night. Stubbs Crow teaches Flying Lessons and Spooksuit Making while Smellybreff is, as always, a small horror! But first they have to tempt back the ghost of Uncle Bigbad… and that proves to be a bit of a problem.

'…will cheer the heart of any child… delightful drawings of canine naughtiness… scary and funny.' *Scotland on Sunday*

ISBN 0 00 675337 X

Collins

An imprint of HarperCollinsPublishers

Little Wolf's Postbag

Ian Whybrow, illustrated by Tony Ross

ARRROOOO!

Calling all readers of Wolf Weekly. Guess who is going to be your new problem page agony nephew? Me. I am Little Wolf really, but you must pretend not knowing. Say 'Dear Mister Helpful' if you want to get a reply printed all poshly in this faymus mag. Because Mister Helpful is my nom de prune (French). So go on, what is up with you? Write quick!

ISBN 0 00 675451 1

Collins

An imprint of HarperCollinsPublishers

Order Form

To order direct from the publishers, just make a list of the
titles you want and fill in the form below:

Name ....

Address ....

....

....

Send to: Dept 6, HarperCollins Publishers Ltd,
Westerhill Road, Bishopbriggs, Glasgow G64 2QT.

Please enclose a cheque or postal order to the value of the
cover price, plus:

UK & BFPO: Add £1.00 for the first book, and 25p per
copy for each additional book ordered.

Overseas and Eire: Add £2.95 service charge. Books will
be sent by surface mail but quotes for airmail despatch
will be given on request.

A 24-hour telephone ordering service is available to
holders of Visa, MasterCard, Amex or Switch cards
on 0141- 772 2281.

An imprint of HarperCollins*Publishers*